WRITTEN AND ILLUSTRATED BY

JEFF WEIGEL

Albert Whitman & Company
Morton Grove, Illinois

Also by Jeff Weigel:
Atomic Ace (He's Just My Dad)

Library of Congress Cataloging-in-Publication Data

Weigel, Jeff, 1958-
Atomic Ace and the robot rampage / written and illustrated by Jeff Weigel.
p. cm.
Summary: As the son of superhero Atomic Ace, a boy is eager for adventures of his own until a horde of robots descends upon his school and he learns that his powers are not yet strong enough to save even himself.
ISBN-13: 978-0-8075-0484-0 (hardcover)
ISBN-10: 0-8075-0484-X (hardcover)
ISBN-13: 978-0-8075-0485-7 (pbk)
ISBN-10: 0-8075-0485-8 (pbk)
[1. Heroes–Fiction. 2. Family life–Fiction. 3. Robots–Fiction. 4. Science fiction. 5. Stories in rhyme.] I. Title.
PZ8.3.W418 Asr 2006 [E]—dc22 2006000003

Published simultaneously in Canada by Fitzhenry & Whiteside, Markham, Ontario.

Printed in China through Colorcraft Ltd., Hong Kong.
10 9 8 7 6 5 4 3 2 1

The line illustrations in this book were produced with ink and brush on Bristol board. The artwork was then scanned and coloring was done electronically in Adobe Photoshop on an Apple Mac G4 Cube. The book was designed by the author and assembled in Adobe InDesign.

For information about Albert Whitman & Company,
please visit our web site at www.albertwhitman.com.

For Kim—just like everything else.

When evil or injustice or disaster threatens Earth,
on land or sea or even out in space,
there's action and adventure and amazing stuff galore
for heroes like my dad: Atomic Ace!

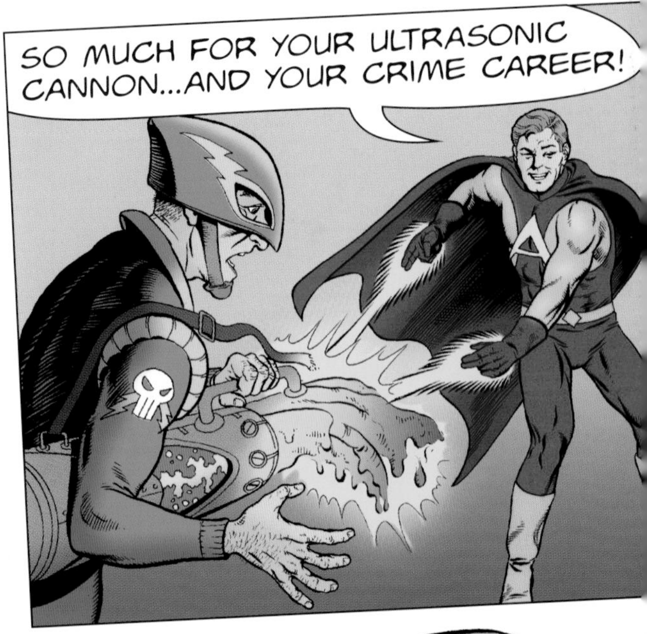

SORRY, SAILOR! THESE SEAS ARE OFF-LIMITS TO WHALERS.

NO REASON AN ENGINE GLITCH SHOULD STOP THIS SHUTTLE MISSION.

Daily Chronicle
Roboconqueror to Be Released from Prison

My dad's been fighting evil since before he married Mom.
He's made a lot of friends and nasty foes.
'Cause when you're foiling bad guys' plans and putting them in jail,
you make enemies—sometimes that's how it goes.

Some kids inherit parents' looks—blue eyes or curly hair,

but family traits like I have are unique.

With practice, I hope someday I'll grow up to be like Dad.

I bet I'll save the Earth most every week!

ATOMIC ACE
NASA Officials Call Atomic Ace to Stop Meteor Threat

My folks say I'm too young to battle evil and fight crime;
instead of stopping crooks, I go to school.
My dad might take a trip to end a threat in outer space,
but Mom and I stay home—not quite so cool.

"Don't worry, dear. I'll handle things until you make it back,"
Mom said today as Dad went on his way.
We watched as he flew up into the early morning sky.
I left to start another boring day.

BY TRACKING THE AURA OF HIS NUCLEAR POWERS, I CAN LOCATE ATOMIC ACE ANYWHERE ON EARTH!
It's just not fair. I'm stuck in school while Dad has all the fun,
like hitting homers somewhere near the moon.
I worked on my assignment, making lists of nouns and verbs,
and hoped my life would get exciting soon.

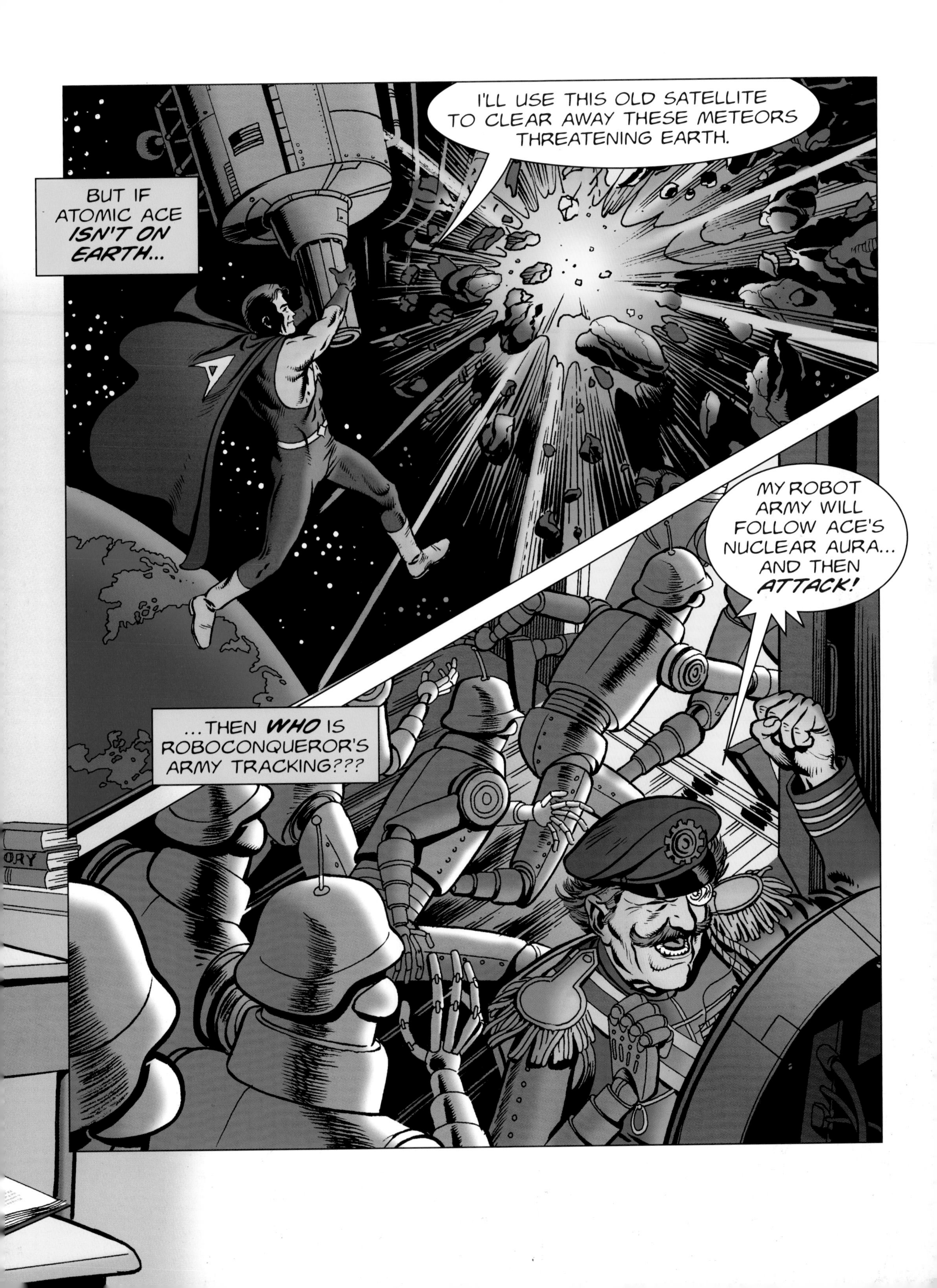
BUT IF ATOMIC ACE ISN'T ON EARTH...
I'LL USE THIS OLD SATELLITE TO CLEAR AWAY THESE METEORS THREATENING EARTH.
MY ROBOT ARMY WILL FOLLOW ACE'S NUCLEAR AURA... AND THEN ATTACK!
...THEN WHO IS ROBOCONQUEROR'S ARMY TRACKING???

Suddenly I heard the sound of heavy, clanking steps.
Looking out the window, I could see
descending on my classroom was a horde of metal men!
Their glowing eyes were looking right at me!

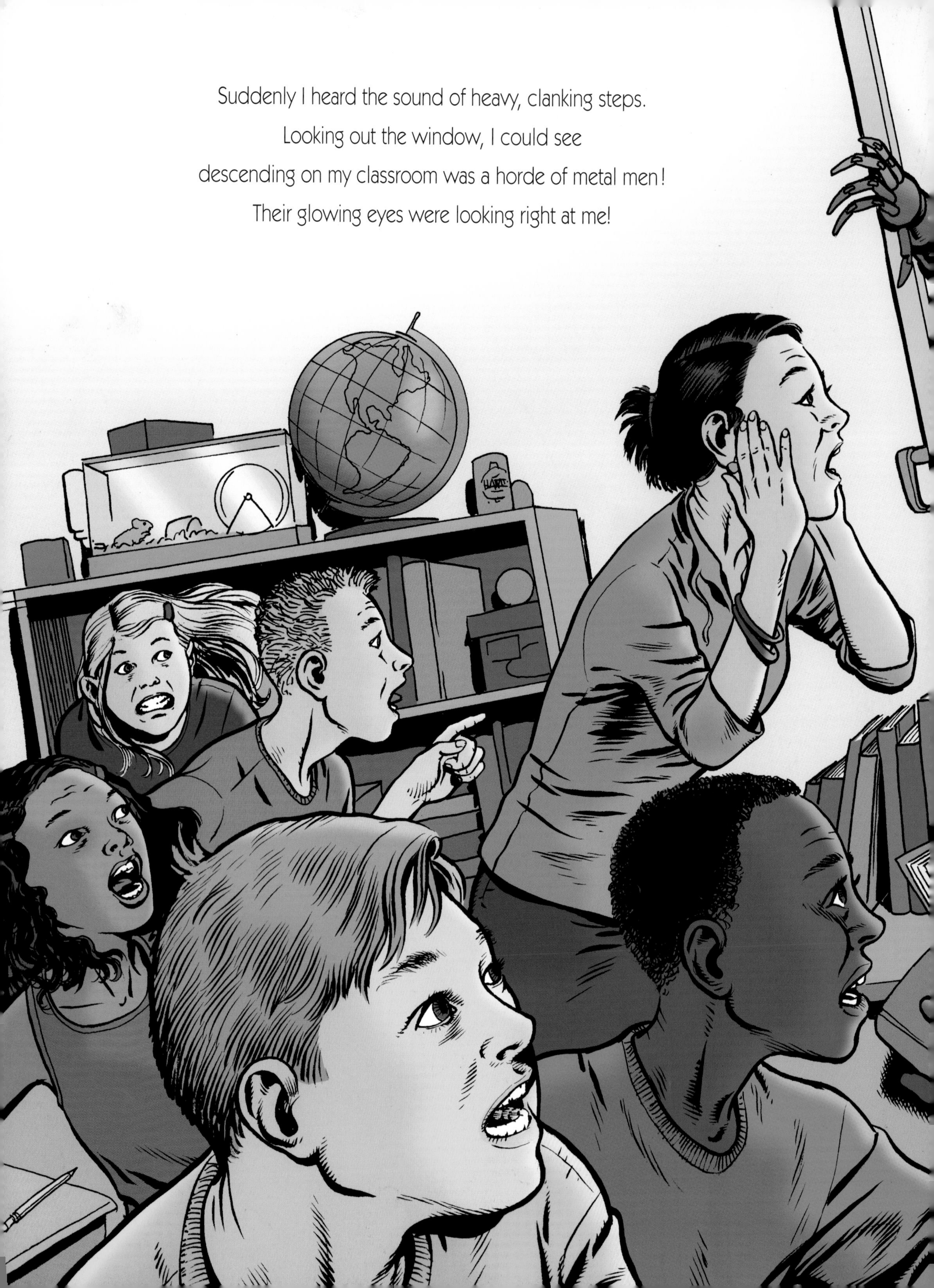

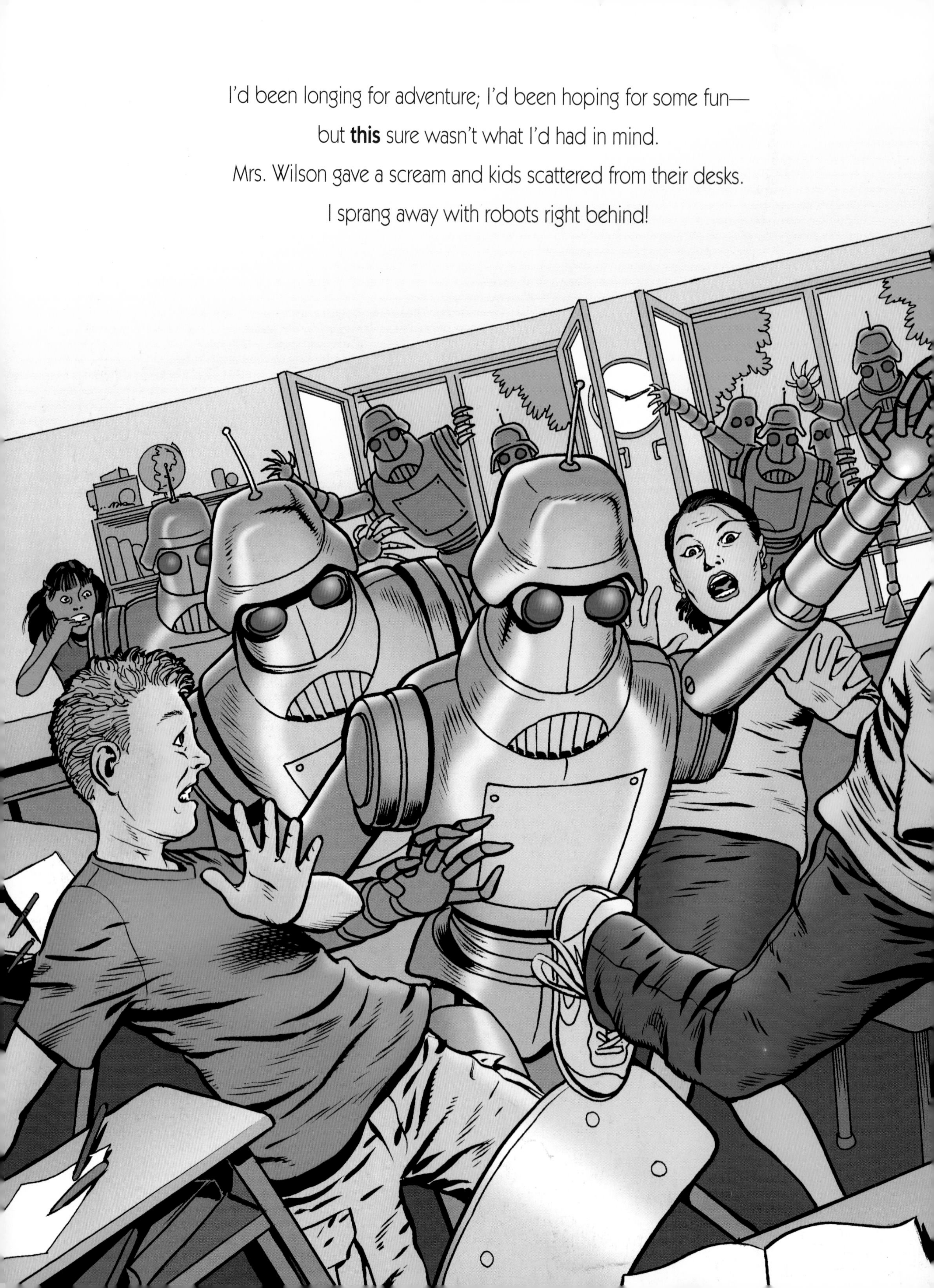

I'd been longing for adventure; I'd been hoping for some fun—
but **this** sure wasn't what I'd had in mind.
Mrs. Wilson gave a scream and kids scattered from their desks.
I sprang away with robots right behind!

MEANWHILE, OUT IN SPACE...
THERE ARE MORE OF THESE METEORS THAN I EXPECTED. THIS JOB COULD TAKE A WHILE.

HA! THE RADAR SHOWS MY ARMY HAS ITS QUARRY SURROUNDED!
...AN ALERT ON MY SUB-SPACE BELT RADIO!
CALLING ATOMIC ACE! A HORDE OF ROBOTS IS ON A RAMPAGE!

I sprinted through an exit, but my troubles just got worse!
Though I shot some sparks and tried to stand my ground,
my powers aren't as strong as Dad's—they didn't help at all!
I panicked as the robots closed around!

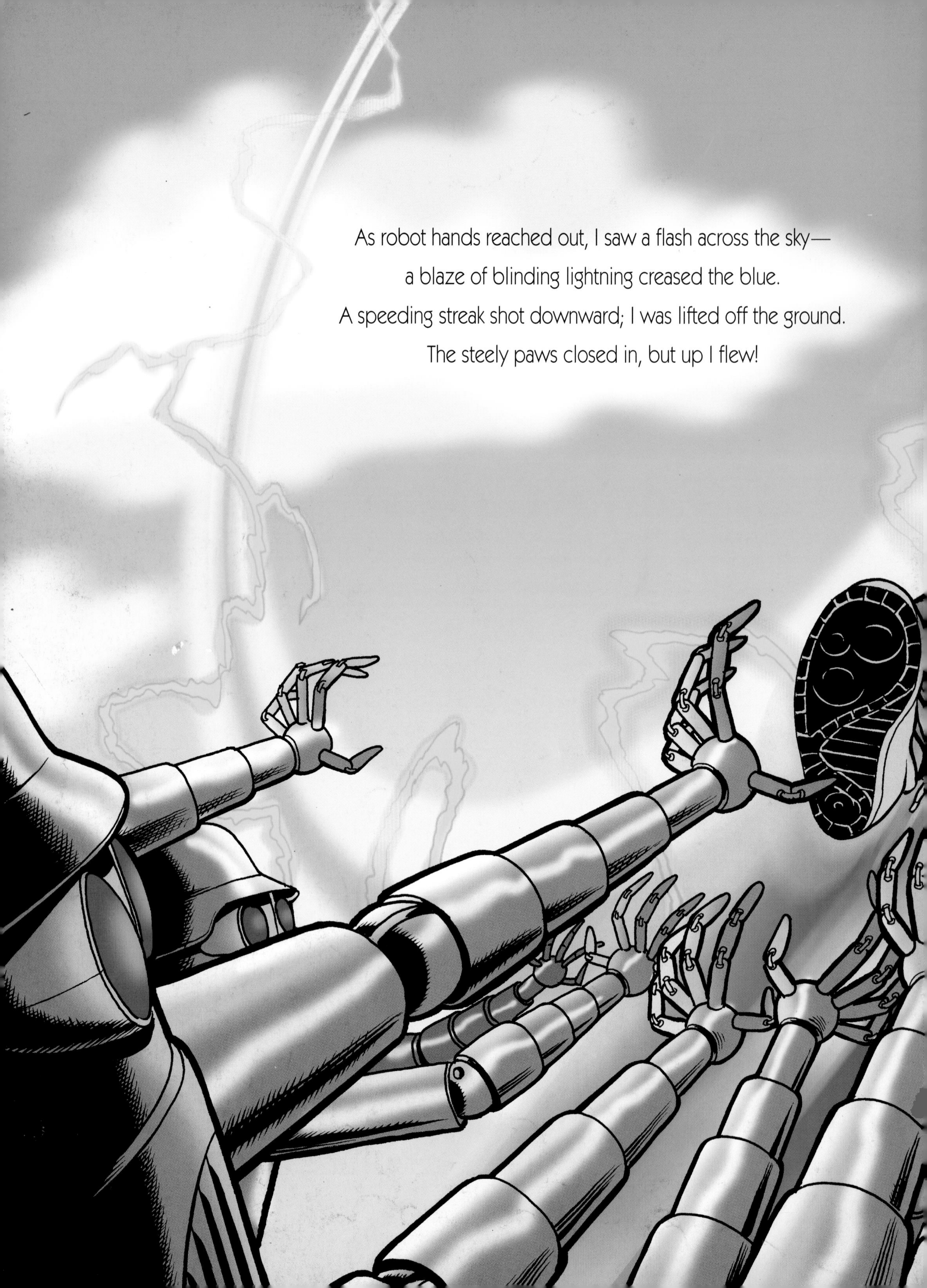

As robot hands reached out, I saw a flash across the sky—
a blaze of blinding lightning creased the blue.
A speeding streak shot downward; I was lifted off the ground.
The steely paws closed in, but up I flew!

I turned to face my rescuer, expecting that I'd see
my hero (and my dad), Atomic Ace.
But someone else had saved me from the evil robot gang—
a hero with a real familiar face!

We'd taken to the sky, but still the mechanoids gave chase.
(I think that losing me had made them mad.)
We took a rest from flying at the first safe place we found,
but up they climbed to reach us—things looked bad!

The robots swarmed the tower just like ants upon a hill;
my rescuer let loose a mighty bolt!
Heads shot sparks and rivets popped! The creatures dropped like flies—
each metal menace scrambled by the jolt!

With all the robots safely fried, we landed on the ground.
I leaped around and shouted, "That was great!"
My mother said, "Your teacher called as I was making lists.
With you in trouble, errands had to wait."

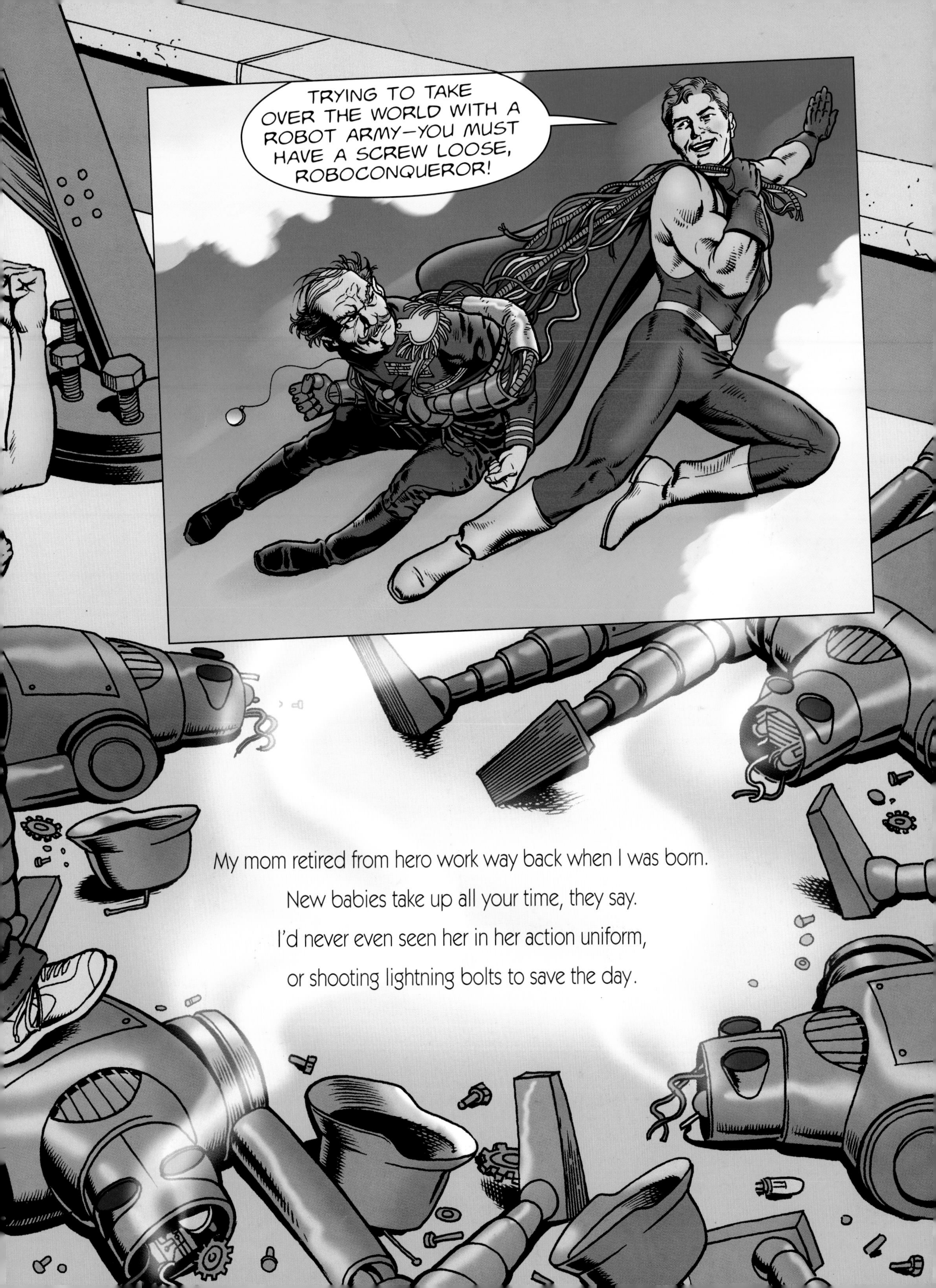

My mom retired from hero work way back when I was born.
New babies take up all your time, they say.
I'd never even seen her in her action uniform,
or shooting lightning bolts to save the day.

YOU'RE TOO LATE, HON. ALL THE EXCITEMENT IS OVER.
YOU SHOULD HAVE SEEN HER, DAD! SHE WAS COOL!

Mom said, "I'm kind of sorry I can't manage to fight crime
on top of all the other things I do."
Dad looked at all the scattered mess; he grinned at Mom and said,
"I know where we can find more help for you."

So these days Mom is saving Earth while Dad stops evil schemes—

we've found a way for things to work out fine.

With everybody pitching in, our home is running smooth.

It's fun to have a family like mine!

evil
evil
evil

THE END